W9-CMU-392

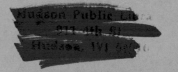

Superhero Max

Lawrence David

illustrated by
Tara Calahan King

A Doubleday Book for Young Readers

For Zachary David
—L.E.D.

To my husband, Rick,
for all your love and support
—T.C.K.

A Doubleday Book for Young Readers
Published by
Random House Children's Books
a division of
Random House, Inc.
1540 Broadway
New York, New York 10036
Doubleday and the anchor with dolphin colophon are registered trademarks of
Random House, Inc.
Text copyright © 2002 by Lawrence David
Illustrations copyright © 2002 by Tara Calahan King

Visit us on the Web! www.randomhouse.com/kids
Educators and librarians, for a variety of teaching tools, visit us at
www.randomhouse.com/teachers
Library of Congress Cataloging-in-Publication Data
David, Lawrence.
Superhero Max / by Lawrence David ; illustrated by Tara Calahan King.
p. cm.
Summary: A second-grade boy has trouble fitting in at his new school, until he wears his
Captain Crusader costume for Halloween.
ISBN: 0-385-32746-3 (trade)
0-385-90851-2 (lib. bdg.)
[1. Schools—Fiction. 2. Play—Fiction. 3. Imagination—Fiction.] I. King, Tara Calahan,
ill. II. Title.
PZ7.D28232 Su 2001
[E]—dc21
99-088212
The text of this book is set in 15-point Symphony.
Book design by Trish Parcell
Manufactured in the United States of America
September 2002
10 9 8 7 6 5 4 3 2 1

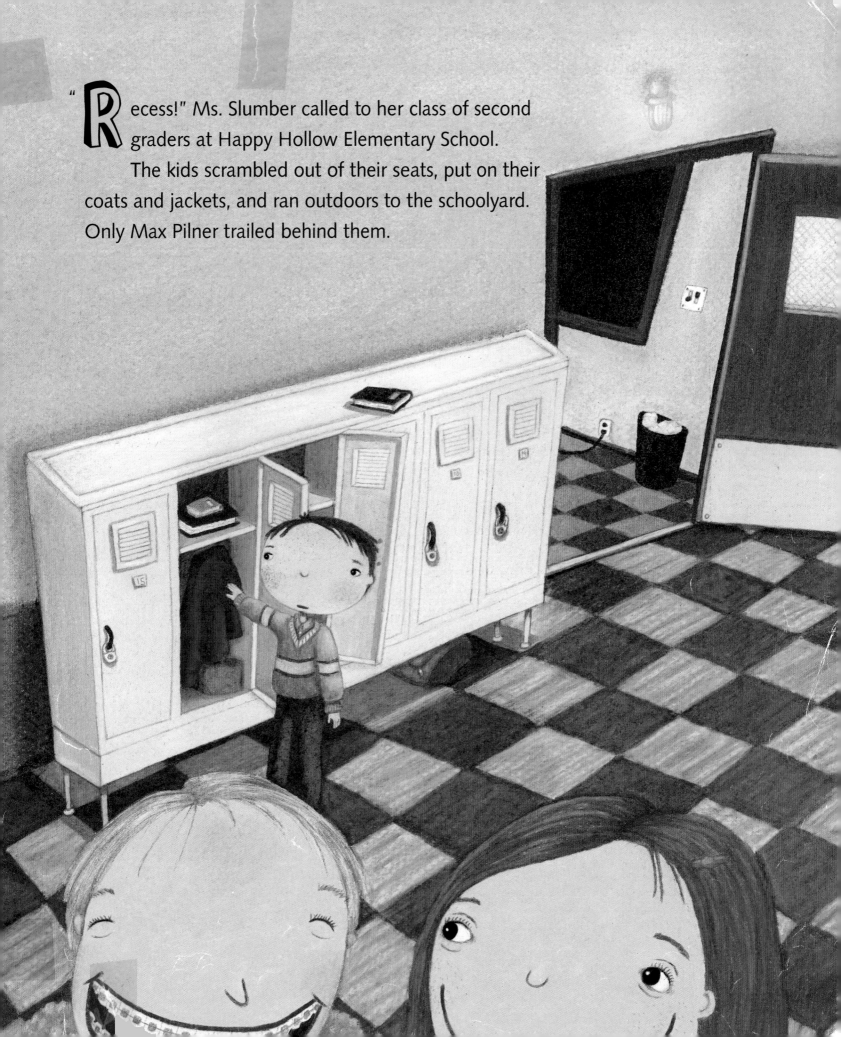

"Recess!" Ms. Slumber called to her class of second graders at Happy Hollow Elementary School.

The kids scrambled out of their seats, put on their coats and jackets, and ran outdoors to the schoolyard. Only Max Pilner trailed behind them.

Max watched as his classmates dashed about.

Some kids played Giant Bug Attack and stomped and clawed and buzzed.

Some kids played Wild Animal Land and squeaked and clucked and roared.

Some kids played Happy Hollow Hospital and yelled and moaned and made siren noises.

Ms. Slumber gave Max a pat on the back. "It's not easy being in a new school, is it?"

Max thought of all his old friends and the games they played at recess.

Max wandered off to the far side of the playground and shut his eyes. He did ten Electric Turnarounds, then opened his eyes and whispered the magic words the kids at his old school said when they played.

"Biffle-Wiffle," Max said.

There was a gigantic flash.

There was a crashing boom.

Max was no longer Max Pilner, second grader at Happy Hollow Elementary School. No, Max Pilner had become Captain Crusader.

biffle-
wiffle

Captain Crusader flew high in the air and saved a plane from crashing into a mountain.

Captain Crusader swam deep beneath the ocean and saved a school of fish from a shark.

Captain Crusader used his supersonic beam to catch the Evil Weevil Gang and put them in jail.

"Recess is over!" Ms. Slumber yelled. "Time to come in."

Max looked around. All the other kids were laughing as they returned to the classroom. Max slowly followed them and took his seat.

"Class," Ms. Slumber announced, "next week, on Halloween, we will dress in costumes and have a spooky celebration. At the end of the day, we'll vote for the most exciting costume."

All the kids whooped and cheered. Max sat quietly at his desk, a small smile spreading across his face.

That entire week after school, Max and his older brother, Billy, worked hard making Max's outfit.

On Halloween, the kids dressed in their costumes.

Some kids were ghosts.

Some kids were cats.

Some kids were ninjas.

And there was even one kid dressed as a llama.

When Max entered the classroom, everyone stopped talking and stared.

Ms. Slumber smiled. "And who is this? I don't recognize him."

Max faced the class. "I'm Captain Crusader," he said. "I have many powers. I fight villains and save animals and people from calamitous disasters."

"Wow," Anne Marie said.

"Cool," George said.

"Neat-o," Brad said.

Max's classmates clapped, and at recess they asked him to join in their games.

Out on the playground, Captain Crusader chased giant bugs back into their dark caves, saved animals from a raging forest fire, and used his supersonic beam to cure all the patients at Happy Hollow Hospital.

Back in the classroom, Max won the award for most exciting costume.

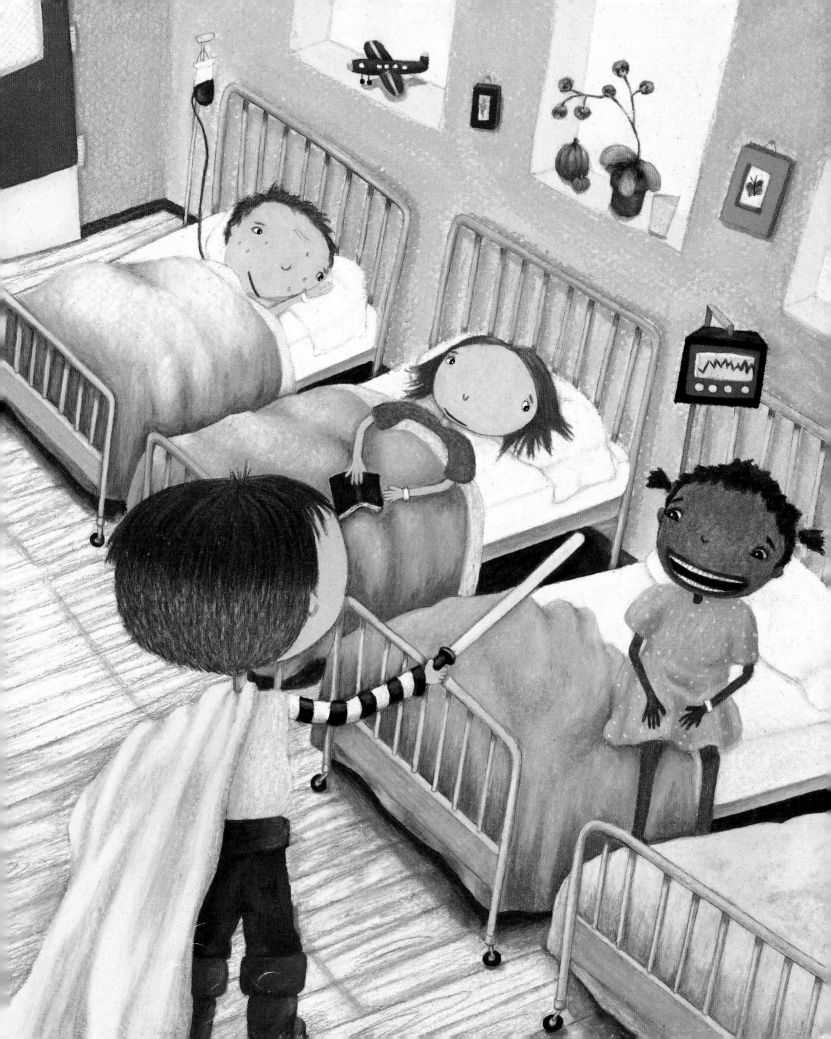

The next day, Max woke up, put on his Captain Crusader costume, and headed downstairs to the kitchen.

Max's dad gave him a puzzled look. "Max, Halloween was yesterday. You're not having another party at school, are you?"

"No, I just like being Captain Crusader," Max told his dad.

"You don't have to wear the costume to be Captain Crusader," Billy said.

Max took his seat and began eating his cereal. "But without my costume, how will the kids know I'm Captain Crusader?" he asked.

The next morning when Max got up for school, the Captain Crusader costume was gone. He ran downstairs to the kitchen. "What happened to my clothes?" he asked his father and brother.

"No more costume," Max's dad said. "From now on Max Pilner is going to school, not Captain Crusader."

Max frowned. His dad took him upstairs to change into plain jeans and a plain shirt.

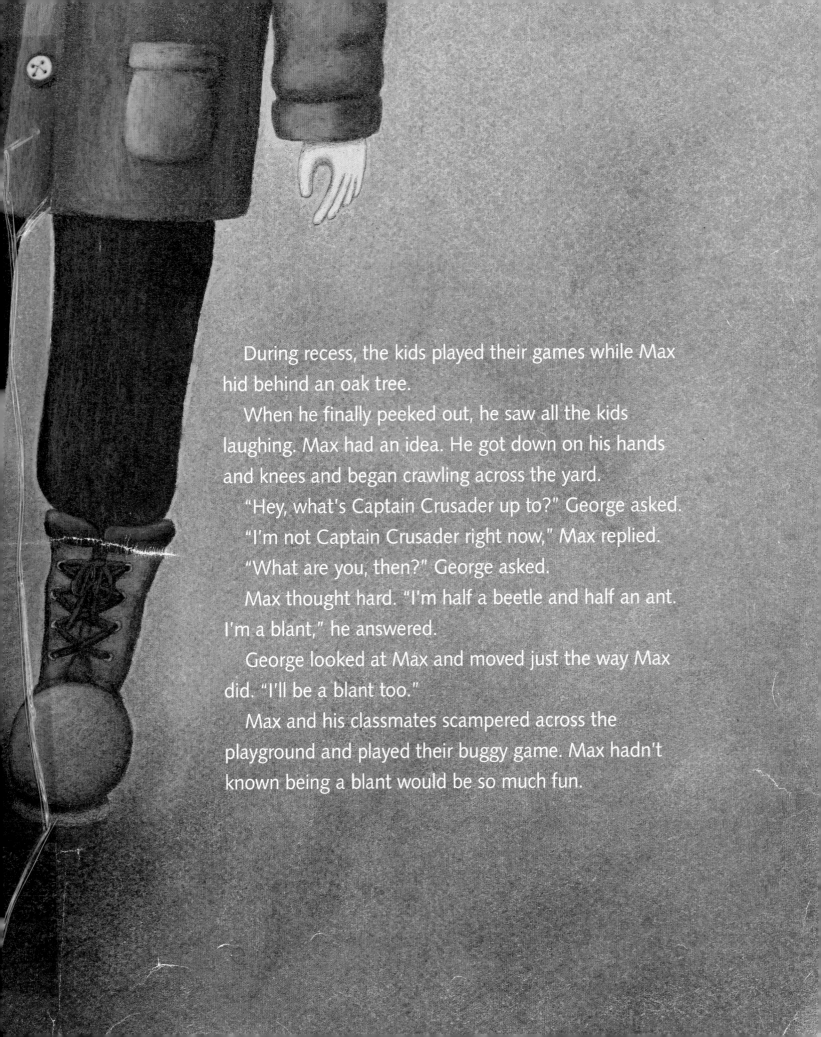

During recess, the kids played their games while Max hid behind an oak tree.

When he finally peeked out, he saw all the kids laughing. Max had an idea. He got down on his hands and knees and began crawling across the yard.

"Hey, what's Captain Crusader up to?" George asked.

"I'm not Captain Crusader right now," Max replied.

"What are you, then?" George asked.

Max thought hard. "I'm half a beetle and half an ant. I'm a blant," he answered.

George looked at Max and moved just the way Max did. "I'll be a blant too."

Max and his classmates scampered across the playground and played their buggy game. Max hadn't known being a blant would be so much fun.

Max Pilner walked home from school that day in his plain jeans and his plain shirt. When he stepped in some mud and got his sneakers dirty, he didn't even notice. He was too busy putting his arms in front of him, pretending to be an elephant with a long trunk. He thought it would be fun to play Wild Animal Land the next day with his friends at school.

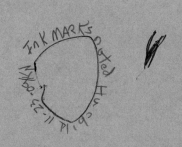

InK MARKs noted Hu
N/Koo 11-23-00 ejN